W9-AQD-771

Hockey

• An Introduction to Being a Good Sport •

by Aaron Derr

illustrations by Jim Kelly

RED
CHAIR
• PRESS •

Start Smart books are published by Red Chair Press

Red Chair Press LLC   PO Box 333   South Egremont, MA 01258-0333
www.redchairpress.com

Publisher's Cataloging-In-Publication Data

Names: Derr, Aaron. | Kelly, Jim, 1949- illustrator.

Title: Hockey : an introduction to being a good sport / by Aaron Derr ; illustrations by
    Jim Kelly.

Description: South Egremont, MA : Red Chair Press, [2017] | Start smart: sports | Interest age
    Description: South Egremont, MA : Red Chair Press, [2017] | Start smart: sports | Interest
    age level: 005-008. | Includes Fast Fact sidebars, a glossary and references for additional
    reading. | Includes bibliographical references and index. | Summary: "Playing a sport is
    good exercise and fun, but being part of a team is more fun for everyone when you know
    the rules of the game and how to be a good sport. Hockey is a popular team sport in North
    America and Europe. In this book, readers learn the history of the game and the role of
    various positions on the ice."-- Provided by publisher.

Identifiers: LCCN 2016934116 | ISBN 978-1-63440-131-9 (library hardcover) |
    ISBN 978-1-63440-137-1 (paperback) | ISBN 978-1-63440-143-2 (ebook)

Subjects: LCSH: Hockey--Juvenile literature. | Sportsmanship--Juvenile literature. | CYAC:
    Hockey. | Sportsmanship.

Classification: LCC GV847.25 .D47 2017 (print) | LCC GV847.25 (ebook) | DDC 796.962--dc23

Illustration credits: cover: Scott Angle; interiors: Jim Kelly; technical charts by Joe LeMonnier

Photo credits: Cover p. 9, 10, 13, 15, 20, 21, 27, 28, 30, 31: Dreamstime; p. 32: Courtesy of the
author, Aaron Derr

This series first published by:
Red Chair Press LLC   PO Box 333   South Egremont, MA 01258-0333

Printed in the United States of America

Distributed in the U.S. by Lerner Publisher Services. www.lernerbooks.com

1116 1P CGBS17

Table of Contents

Words in **bold type** are defined in the glossary.

CHAPTER 1

New Lineup

Ever since Matthew, J.J. and Nate started playing ice hockey, they've played on the same team: the Wolves.

They're perfect teammates. They always seem to know what the other is thinking. Sometimes Matthew makes a perfect pass and J.J. scores a goal. Other times J.J. makes the pass and Nate scores the goal.

In hockey, players **substitute** while the game is going on. This is called a line change.

Matthew, J.J. and Nate have always been on the same **line**. When one of them came off the ice, so did the others. And when one came back on, so did the others.

But on the first day of practice before this season, everything changed.

"Matthew, I'm going to move you to a different line," their coach said. "J.J. and Nate will skate with our brand new player, Carter."

Uh-oh. Matthew did not like this at all.

CHAPTER 2

Working on Offense

Most hockey teams have one goalie, two defensemen and three forwards on the ice at the same time. Last season, Matthew, J.J. and Nate were the forwards on the first line.

But now their coach was moving Matthew to a different line and replacing him with Carter, the new kid!

"The best hockey teams have good players on every line," their coach said. "The second line is just as important as the first line."

"But I want to be on the same line as J.J. and Nate!" Matthew said.

"Matthew, I need you to be a good team player," said their coach. "Now let's get to work."

In order to score goals in hockey, your team has to be able to pass the puck. It's very hard for one player to skate all the way down the ice by himself without losing the puck to the other team.

"OK guys," their coach says. "Let's work on our passing."

For their first **drill**, J.J. started in the middle of the ice, with Nate on one side and Carter, the new kid, on the other.

Since J.J. started off with the puck, it was up to her to decide which teammate to pass to.

All three players began to skate down the ice. J.J. kept the puck close so the defense couldn't get it.

But at the same time, three of their teammates were playing defense and trying to stop them.

J.J. had a choice: pass to her friend Nate or the new kid Carter.

Carter was wide open on one side. Nate had a defender right next to him on the other. J.J. passed the puck to Carter, and Carter scored a goal!

"Great job, guys," said their coach. "Way to work together."

But Matthew did not like it at all.

Most hockey teams use six players at a time.

Goaltender: The goalie usually stays right in front of the net. He wears a different mask from his teammates to protect him from those fast-flying pucks!

Defensemen: These two players are usually the first ones to fall back to help the goalie. They can skate all the way down the rink but don't usually get too close to the other team's goal.

Forwards: While these three players often come back to help the defensemen, they also skate all the way down the rink and try to score right in front of the other team's goal. That's a lot of skating! Most teams use one player at center and two players at wing: a left wing and right wing.

Note: Left and right is always from the view of the Goalie.

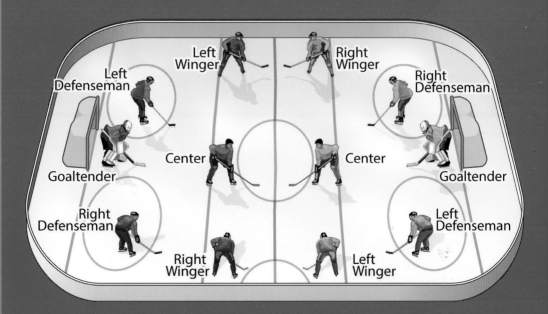

Working on Defense

During a break in practice, J.J. and Nate sat down next to Matthew.

"Hey, that new kid is pretty good," Nate said. "You should give him a chance."

"Not as good as me!" said Matthew, and then he got back on the ice to practice with his new line.

After the Wolves were done working on their offense, they started working on playing defense.

"You can't have a good hockey team if you don't play good defense," their coach said.

Playing defense in hockey is tricky for one big reason: You have to skate backwards!

Even though some players are called "defensemen" and other players are called "forwards," everybody in hockey plays defense.

FUN FACT

Most hockey leagues use officials to enforce the rules. Watch out! They will call a **penalty** if you break a rule.

J.J., Carter and Nate got in line and practiced skating backwards. Their job was to keep the puck away from the goal.

When you're playing defense, you have to work together. If the puck gets past one of your teammates, you may have to go help him out.

JUST JOKING!

Q: What do hockey players catch after an extra-long game?

A: Their breath!

When you commit a penalty in hockey, you may have to go sit in the penalty box, and your team has to play **short-handed**. When one team is allowed more players on the ice than the other, it's called a power play.

Since Carter was the new guy, he didn't always know where to go.

On their first try, the offense got past J.J., and Carter wasn't able to help until they had scored a goal.

"That wouldn't have happened if I was out there," said Matthew from his spot on the bench.

Carter was sad. Even though it was only practice, he had made a mistake and let the offense score.

Nate and J.J. skated over to him. "It's OK, Carter," J.J. said. "Yeah," said Nate. "You'll get the hang of it. Just keep trying your best."

That made Carter feel better.

The next time, the offense passed the puck past Nate, but Carter knew just where to go. He skated over and knocked the puck away from the goal.

"Great play, Carter!" their coach said.

"I could have done that, too," said Matthew.

CHAPTER 4

Their Best Shots

Before their next practice, J.J. and Nate sat down to talk with Matthew.

"Hey Matthew," Nate said. "The new guy Carter is a really good player."

"Yeah," said J.J. "And he's really nice, too. I think you'd like him if you give him a chance."

"Right," Nate said. "He's one of our teammates, so we should all be nice to him."

Matthew didn't say anything at first, but he knew his friends were right. Teammates must always treat each other with respect.

He decided he should be nicer to Carter. Even though he wanted to be on the ice at the same time as J.J. and Nate, he could still have fun playing on another line. And he could still do his part to help his team.

"OK," said Matthew. "I'll give him one chance."

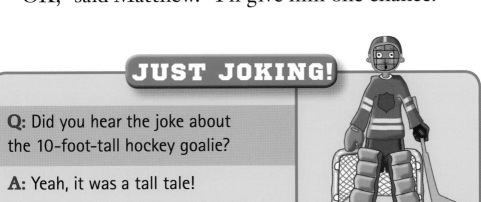

JUST JOKING!

Q: Did you hear the joke about the 10-foot-tall hockey goalie?

A: Yeah, it was a tall tale!

In professional baseball, basketball and football, championship teams get to keep their trophies. But in the NHL, winners only keep the Stanley Cup until a new team wins the championship! The Montreal Canadiens have won the Cup 24 times, more than any other team.

At this practice, the Wolves were working on shooting.

All of the players lined up in a row and worked on **snap shots**. Carter was having trouble getting it right, so Matthew skated over to help.

"You've almost got it, Carter," Matthew said. "Just remember to keep your head down, and don't look up until after your stick hits the puck."

"Thanks Matthew," Carter said. He took Matthew's advice and tried again. It worked!

Next, the Wolves worked on their **wrist shots**. Carter was really good at wrist shots, but he noticed that Matthew was having trouble.

"Hey Matthew," Carter said. "Wrist shots are easier for me when I just flick the stick nice and easy."

Matthew tried it, and it worked! He ripped a great wrist shot right at the goal.

"Wow," Matthew said. "Thanks Carter."

FUN FACT

The National Hockey League (NHL) is the most popular professional hockey league in the United States and Canada. There are 30 teams, and the champion at the end of the year is awarded the Stanley Cup, an actual cup that is more than 35 inches tall and weighs nearly 35 pounds!

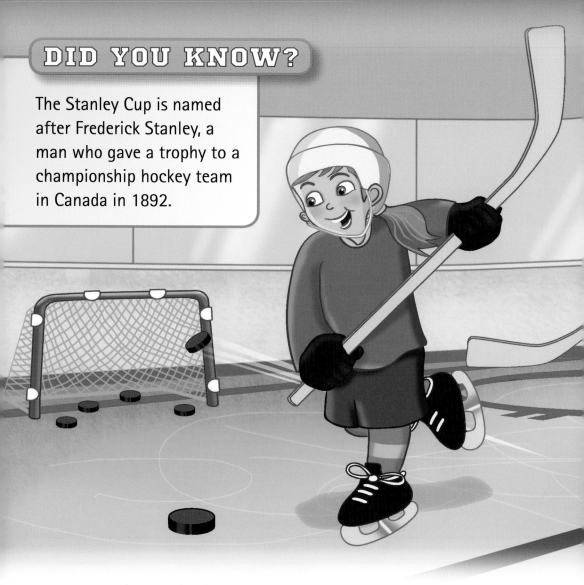

The Stanley Cup is named after Frederick Stanley, a man who gave a trophy to a championship hockey team in Canada in 1892.

At the end of practice, the Wolves worked on **slap shots**. Matthew and Carter were doing great, but J.J. and Nate were having trouble.

"Hey Carter," Matthew said. "Let's go help out J.J. and Nate." Carter and Matthew skated over to where J.J and Nate were practicing.

"Hey guys," Matthew said. "When you're taking a slap shot, remember that your stick should actually hit the ice right behind the puck."

"Yeah," Carter said. "And remember that you shouldn't swing too hard until you get the hang of it."

Before long, all four players were doing great!

CHAPTER 5

Game On

Before the first game of the season, Matthew sat down next to J.J. and Nate.

"Hey guys," Matthew said. "Carter is a really nice guy. And he's a good hockey player, too. We're lucky to have him on our team." J.J. and Nate looked at each other and smiled.

When the game started. J.J., Nate and Carter started on the same line. Matthew cheered them on from the bench. "Go get 'em, guys!" Matthew yelled.

After a few minutes, J.J., Nate and Carter started to get tired. All three of them skated toward the bench. Matthew and two other players skated out to take their turn.

"Go Matthew!" Carter said. "You can do it!"

The Wolves won the game 5–4. Carter scored two goals. Matthew didn't score a goal but he did make a great pass to help one of his teammates score.

JUST JOKING!

Q: Why was the astronaut so bad at hockey?

A: He kept staring off into space!

After the game, all of players slapped high fives and celebrated their win. "Great game!" they all said.

Then their coach had the players gather around him. "Great job, guys," he said. "I'm proud of you all for winning the game.

"But most of all, I'm proud of you all for being such good teammates." Then he looked at Matthew and winked.

The first step to learning ice hockey is learning how to skate. Once you're on the ice wearing a pair of skates, bend your knees while keeping your head and chest up. Keep your feet about shoulder-width apart. Push out and back with one leg while gliding on the other. Then switch it up. Practice stopping by turning both skates at an angle and pushing the **blades** against the ice. Practice this until you get comfortable, then start skating with a hockey stick. Once you feel good about that, start pushing the puck around the ice. Always work to keep your head and chest up. You can't play hockey if you're constantly looking at the puck, so work on being able to control the puck while looking up.

Glossary

blade: the flat, long part of the skate the glides along the ice

carving: a design cut from rock or other hard material

drill: the part of practice when you work on the same part of the game over and over again

Egypt: a country in northeastern Africa

line: a group of players who always play together

penalty: when a hockey player breaks the rules and must sit out of the game

power play: when a hockey team is allowed to play with one more player than the other team because of a penalty

short-handed: when a hockey team has to play with fewer players because of a penalty

slap shot: when the player brings the stick way back and swings it at the puck to knock it toward the goal

snap shot: when the player shoots the puck at the goal by bringing the stick back to about knee height and snapping it forward quickly so that it knocks the puck forward

substitute: when one player is replaced with another during a game

wrist shot: when the player shoots the puck at the goal by barely bringing the stick back at all and instead flicking the puck forward using mostly his wrists

What Did You Learn?

See how much you learned about hockey. Answer *true* or *false* for each statement below. Write your answers on a separate piece of paper.

1 In hockey, the game stops every time the players substitute.
True or false?

2 Most hockey teams have three forwards on the ice at one time.
True or false?

3 A power play is when one team must play with fewer players than the other.
True or false?

4 NHL stands for Normal Hockey League.
True or false?

5 The NHL's championship trophy is called the Stanley Trophy.
True or false?

Answers: 1. False (Players can substitute while the game is still being played.), 2. True, 3. True, 4. False. (NHL stands for National Hockey League.), 5. False. (the trophy is actually called the Stanley Cup.)

For More Information

Books

Biskup, Agnieszka. *Hockey: How It Works* (The Science of Sports Series), Capstone Press, 2010.

Editors, SI for Kids. *The Top 10 Lists of Everything in Hockey.* Time Inc Books, 2015.

Editors, Sports Illustrated. *Hockey's Greatest.* Sports Illustrated Books, 2015.

Zweig, Eric. *Great Goalies* (Hockey Hall of Fame Kids Series). Firefly Books, 2014.

Places

Hockey Hall of Fame, Toronto, Ontario. Home of the Stanley Cup and all major NHL trophies. Includes replica Montreal Canadiens' dynasty-era dressing room, and interactive exhibits.

U.S. Hockey Hall of Fame and Museum, Eveleth, Minnesota. Celebrate the history of American hockey with the "Great Wall of Fame" displaying inductee plaques, historical displays representing all levels of U.S. hockey, video presentations, interactive experiences.

Web Sites

The official site of the Hockey Hall of Fame with photos, statistics of the greatest players. Great moments in NHL history, women's hockey, and Winter Olympics.
htpps://www.hhof.com

Complete overview of Team USA with youth hockey rules and regulations.
www.USAhockey.com/youthhockey

Official home of the National Hockey League. News, teams and player profiles.
www.nhl.com

Note to educators and parents: Our editors have carefully reviewed these web sites to ensure they are suitable for children. Web sites change frequently, however, and we cannot guarantee that a site's future contents will continue to meet our high standards of quality and educational value. You may wish to preview these sites and closely supervise children whenever they access the Internet.

Index

About the Author

Aaron Derr Aaron Derr is a writer based just outside of Dallas, Texas. He has more than 15 years of experience writing and editing magazines and books for kids of all ages. When he's not reading or writing, Aaron enjoys watching and playing sports, and being a good sport with his wife and two kids.

DATE DUE

			PRINTED IN U.S.A.